Shhh! Don't Wake the Royal Baby!

by Martha Mumford

illustrated by
Ada Grey

BLOOMSBURY
LONDON NEW DELHI NEW YORK SYDNEY

The Royal Palace was in chaos.

The Royal Baby just
would not go to sleep.

The Duchess rocked the baby gently
but as soon as she lowered the
little one into the crib . . .

Waaaaaaah!

the baby woke up again.

The Duke tried taking the baby for a whirr in his helicopter, which worked for a while, but as soon as the helicopter landed . . .

Waaaaaaaah!

the baby was off again.

Even the ancestral golden royal dummy didn't work.

Waaaaaaah!

Waaaaaaah!

Waaaaaaah!

Waaaaaaah!

Waaaaaaah!

Waaaaaaaah!

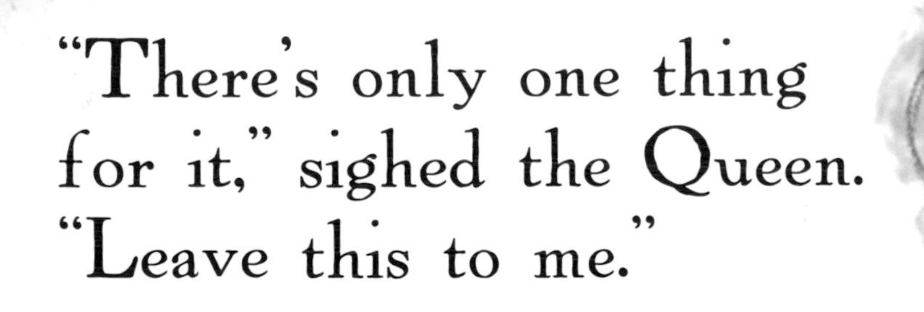

"There's only one thing for it," sighed the Queen. "Leave this to me."

Outside in the palace gardens
Pearl II, the Queen's private jet,
was revving up its engines.
The Queen jumped on board and –

WHOOSH!

The plane soared
through the air.

"Look!" said the Queen, trying to distract the baby by pointing out the fluffy clouds below them.

But the Royal Baby just kept on crying.

"OK, sweetpea," cried the Queen, "hold tight!" With that, the Queen opened the aircraft door, pressed the eject button and leapt out of the plane.

GERONIMO!

As her parachute unfolded and they gently floated to ground, the Royal Baby finally fell asleep.

Everyone gathered around the crib
and gazed lovingly at the darling baby,
sleeping peacefully. What a treasure!

Just then, the King strode in.
"Bravo!" he cried. "It worked. Three cheers for the Queen. Hip, hip, hooray. Hip, hip . . ."

"Shhh!" cried the Duchess.
"Don't wake the Royal Baby!"

But it was too late.

Waaaaaaaah!

Waaaaaaaah!

Waaaaaaaaah!

All eyes were suddenly upon the Queen. "There's only so much parachuting one can do at my age," she said. "You'll just have to try rocking the crib instead.

So the King rocked the crib gently and sang:

"Rockabye Royal Baby, please fall asleep,
the noise is deafening so don't make a peep."

Soon the Royal Baby was fast asleep again. Everyone sighed with relief. But then, just below the nursery window . . .

"LEFT, RIGHT, LEFT, RIGHT, AT EASE!"

bellowed the sergeant major.
It was the changing of the guard.

“Shhh!” cried the Duke.
“Don’t wake the
Royal Baby!”

But it was too late.

Waaaaaaah!
Waaaaaaaah!
Waaaaaaaaah!

"Don't worry," said the Duke.
"I'll read a story. That will do the trick.

Once upon a time, in a beautiful palace, there lived . . ."

And, before he had chance to say,

"They all lived happily ever after."

the Royal Baby was dreaming sweet dreams.

Until . . .

YIP-YAP,
YIP-YAP,
WOOF,
WOOF,
WOOF,
WOOF!

The Royal Dog Handler was taking the corgis for a walk in the palace gardens.

"Shhh!" cried the Queen. "Don't wake the Royal Baby!"
But it was too late.
Waaaaaaaah!
Waaaaaaaaah!
Waaaaaaaaah!

Then came an even noisier kerfuffle . . .

"What on earth . . ."
bellowed the Duke, "is that?"

Busy in the banqueting hall, the baby's auntie and uncle were preparing the most lavish party to celebrate the new arrival.

"More blinis! We need more blinis!" called the baby's auntie.

"Hip hop, dance or pop?" cried the baby's uncle over the booming noise from the loud speakers.

"SHHH!" cried the Duke. "You're waking the Royal Baby!"

"Enough!" said the Duchess. "Everybody out! All this noise and fussing is not helping one little bit. This baby needs peace and quiet, and a cuddle from Mummy and Daddy."

And she was right – that was **just** what the baby needed!

Later that day, snores echoed from all around the Palace. And the loudest snores of all? Well they came from the nursery.

Shhh! Don't wake the Royal Family!

For everyone at Bloomsbury Children's Books – MM

For Ava, Vicki and Emma – AG

Bloomsbury Publishing, London, New Delhi, New York and Sydney

First published in Great Britain in 2013 by Bloomsbury Publishing Plc
50 Bedford Square, London, WC1B 3DP

A CIP catalogue record for this book is available from the British Library

ISBN 978 1 4088 4463 2

Printed in Belgium by Proust, Turnhout

1 3 5 7 9 10 8 6 4 2

www.bloomsbury.com